To Bob with love
— Margaret Ryan

For Daniel, Niall, and Katharine
— David Melling

Smiler, the crocodile,
had a toothache.

He had a
toothache
when he ate.

He had a
toothache
when he
drank.

He even had
a toothache
when he smiled.

"This toothache really hurts,"
he groaned.
"OOH . . . AAH . . . OOH."

He waddled out of the river onto
the bank and groaned again.
"OOH . . . AAH . . . OOH."

Up in the trees, Bumpy,
the sun bear, heard a noise.
She bumped down onto the
riverbank to find out what
was wrong.

"What's the matter, Smiler?"
she asked. "Do you have a
tummyache? Sometimes I get
a tummyache when I eat
too much honey."

"No," groaned
Smiler. "It's not
a tummyache.
Crocodiles don't
eat too much. It's a
toothache. Look in my
mouth, Bumpy. See if you can
find the sore tooth."

Bumpy looked in Smiler's mouth. There were lots of big teeth in there.

She put her paw in and wiggled a front one. It was all right. It didn't hurt.

She put her paw in and wiggled a back one. It was all right. It didn't hurt, either.

She put her paw in and wiggled
two more teeth. But she couldn't
find the sore one.

"You are so lazy, Smiler," said
Bumpy. "Don't you ever brush
your teeth? I can see last week's
dinner still on them."
But Smiler just groaned again,
louder.
"OOH . . . AAH . . . OOH."

Up in the trees, Rainbow, the parrot, heard the noise. She flew down to the riverbank to find out what was wrong.

"What's the matter, Smiler?" she asked. "Do you have a beak-ache? Sometimes I get a beak-ache when I talk too much."

"No," groaned Smiler. "I don't
have a beak, you silly bird. And
crocodiles don't talk too much.
It's a toothache. Look in my
mouth, Rainbow. See if you can
find the sore tooth."

Rainbow looked in Smiler's mouth. There were lots of big teeth in there.

She put her beak in and wiggled a front one. It was all right. It didn't hurt.

She put her beak in and wiggled a back one. It was all right. It didn't hurt, either.

She put her beak in and wiggled
three more teeth. But she
couldn't find the sore one.

"You are so lazy, Smiler," she said. "Don't you ever brush your teeth? I can see last month's dinner still on them."
But Smiler just groaned again, even louder. "OOH . . . AAH . . . OOH."

Up in the trees, Fuzzbuzz, the little orangutan, heard the noise. He swung down to the riverbank to find out what was wrong.

"What's the matter, Smiler?" he asked. "Do you have an arm-ache? Sometimes I get an arm-ache when I swing from the trees too much."

"No," groaned Smiler. "It's not an arm-ache. Crocodiles don't swing from the trees. It's a toothache. Look in my mouth, Fuzzbuzz. See if you can find the sore tooth."

Fuzzbuzz looked in Smiler's mouth. There were lots of big teeth in there.

He put his hand in and wiggled a front one. It was all right. It didn't hurt.

He put his hand in and wiggled a back one. It was all right. It didn't hurt, either.

He put his hand in and wiggled
four more teeth. But he couldn't
find the sore one.

"You are so lazy, Smiler," he said.
"Don't you ever brush your teeth?
I can see last year's dinner still
on them."

Fuzzbuzz put his hand back into
Smiler's mouth and was
wiggling another big tooth
in the back when they
heard a noise. . . .

"WE'RE LEAN, WE'RE MEAN,
WE'RE VERY, VERY KEEN
TO STING ANY PART OF YOU
THAT CAN BE SEEN!"

And marching out of the bat
cave came . . .

"The Angry Ant Gang," cried
Smiler. "Well, they won't
sting me. I'm going
back down to the river."

And he shut his mouth with a
loud SNAP.

"Ow," yelled Fuzzbuzz, and
got his hand out just in time.

"OOH . . . AAH." Smiler began to
groan again, then he stopped.

"That's funny," he said.
"My toothache's gone away."
"That's because I have your sore
tooth." Fuzzbuzz grinned.

"Look. When I pulled out my hand, I pulled out your sore tooth, too."

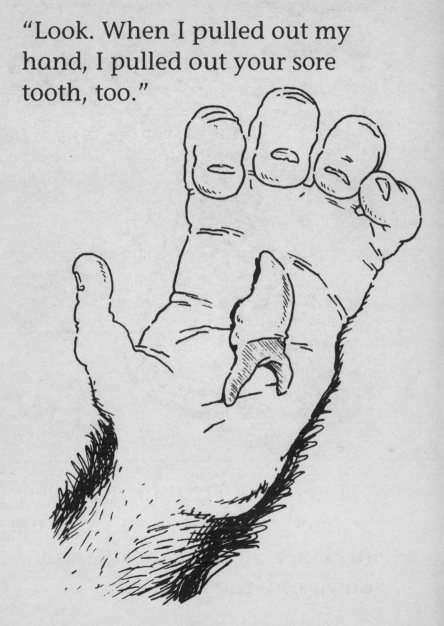

"Thank you, Fuzzbuzz." Smiler
grinned. "That feels much better."
And he waddled quickly back
down into the river.

Fuzzbuzz climbed quickly to the top of his tree. "You'll remember to brush your teeth now, won't you, Smiler?" he called.

"Oh, yes," said Smiler. "I'll remember."

Rainbow flew quickly to the
top of her tree.
"You won't forget, will you,
Smiler?" she called.

"Oh, no," said Smiler.
"I won't forget."

Bumpy climbed quickly to the
top of her tree.
"Do you promise, Smiler?"
she called.

"I promise," said Smiler.

Then they all grinned as the
Angry Ant Gang marched past
muttering . . .

"YOU GOT AWAY THIS TIME,
BUT WE WILL BE BACK.
WE'LL GET YOU NEXT TIME
WE WANT A SNACK!"

The next day, the jungle friends
went down to the river.
"We'll see if Smiler has brushed
his teeth yet," they said.

They found Smiler snoozing in the sun on the riverbank.

"Have you brushed last week's dinner off your teeth yet, Smiler?" asked Bumpy.

"Sort of." Smiler grinned.

"Have you brushed last month's dinner off your teeth yet, Smiler?" asked Rainbow.

"In a way."
Smiler grinned.

"Have you
brushed last
year's dinner
off your teeth
yet, Smiler?"
asked Fuzzbuzz.

"Almost."
Smiler grinned.

Then he opened his mouth wide
and all the little jungle birds
flew in and out, in and out.

They pecked
at the food
from Smiler's
front teeth.
PECK, PECK,
PECK.

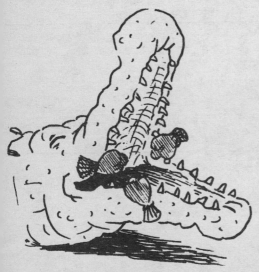

They pecked
at the food from
Smiler's back
teeth. PECK,
PECK, PECK.

They peck peck pecked the food
from all the rest of Smiler's teeth.

The jungle friends watched in amazement.

Smiler grinned. "This is how
lazy crocodiles brush their teeth,"
he said.